D0842436

E
O

Old, Wendie.

Stacy had a little
sister.

$13.95

DATE			

DISCARD

MAR -- 1995

PRINCE GEORGE PUBLIC LIBRARY
887 DOMINION STREET
PRINCE GEORGE, B.C. V2L 5L1
563-9251

BAKER & TAYLOR BOOKS

Stacy Had A Little Sister

Wendie C. Old
Illustrated by Judith Friedman

Albert Whitman & Company
Morton Grove, Illinois

PRINCE GEORGE PUBLIC LIBRARY

For my mother,
and all the mothers in the world who worry.
W.O.

With all my thanks to
Mark, Shannon, Daniel, and Matthew.
J.F.

Library of Congress Cataloging-in-Publication Data
Old, Wendie C.
Stacy had a little sister / Wendie C. Old;
illustrated by Judith Friedman.
p. cm.
Summary: Stacy has mixed feelings about her new sister
Ashley, but when the baby dies of sudden infant death
syndrome, Stacy is sad and misses her.
ISBN 0-8075-7598-4
[1. Babies—Fiction. 2. Death—Fiction. 3. Sudden
infant death syndrome—Fiction. 4. Sisters—Fiction.]
I. Friedman, Judith, 1945- ill. II. Title.
PZ7.04514St 1995   94-14537
[E]—dc20   CIP
                                                AC

The text typeface is Caxton Book.
The illustration medium is watercolor.
Design by Eileen Mueller Neill.

Text © 1995 by Wendie C. Old.
Illustrations © 1995 by Judith Friedman.
Published in 1995 by Albert Whitman & Company,
6340 Oakton Street, Morton Grove, Illinois 60053.
Published simultaneously in Canada by
General Publishing, Limited, Toronto.
All rights reserved. No part of this book may be
reproduced or transmitted in any form or by any means,
electronic or mechanical, including photocopying,
recording, or by any information storage and retrieval
system, without permission in writing from the
publisher. Printed in the United States of America.
10 9 8 7 6 5 4 3 2 1

A Note for Parents

Sudden Infant Death Syndrome is the major cause of death for infants between one week and one year of age. Unfortunately, its cause or causes are unknown.

When a new baby dies, parents are overcome by shock and grief. The children in the family are shocked and sad, too. And siblings may feel confused and guilty, wondering if somehow they have caused the baby to die. It is important for parents to share simple, honest information with their children and to be affectionate towards them, providing a reassurance that words cannot.

Medical researchers do continue to run many studies, and have already accumulated much knowledge on SIDS. Several areas are being studied, such as the brain, the heart, sleeping positions, and environmental factors. It is likely that eventually several causes will be found to explain SIDS.

It *is* known that SIDS occurs most frequently in infants two to four months old. And death occurs within seconds, so the baby does not suffer. Though SIDS cannot be prevented, good prenatal care is essential to increasing a baby's chances for good health, and it *may* lower the risk of SIDS. SIDS is *not* caused by suffocation or aspiration. It is neither contagious nor hereditary. And SIDS occurs in all social, economic, ethnic, and racial groups in the United States.

The Sudden Infant Death Syndrome Alliance is a coalition of more than fifty national organizations. It supports medical research, and works to provide current, reliable information on SIDS. To contact the alliance, write: *Sudden Infant Death Syndrome Alliance; 10500 Little Patuxent Parkway; Suite 420; Columbia, MD 21044. Phone: (800)221-SIDS or (410)964-8000.*

Stacy had a little sister.

Daddy took pictures of her at the hospital after she was born. He brought them home to show Stacy and Gramma.

"This is your new sister," he said. "Her name is Ashley. Isn't she beautiful?"

Daddy gave Stacy her very own Ashley picture to keep.

Stacy stared at the picture. She thought Ashley didn't look like much—just a tiny red face peeking out of a blanket.

"Can't she open her eyes yet?" Stacy asked.

"She was sleeping when I took the pictures," Daddy explained. "But when she opens those eyes, you'll find they're the bluest blue you've ever seen."

Stacy looked at that picture a long time. She wasn't sure she liked this new baby.

At bedtime Stacy crumpled the picture up into a ball and threw it under her bed.

Stacy missed her mommy. Gramma's bedtime story and goodnight kiss just weren't the same as Mommy's. She wondered when Mommy would come home.

The next day Daddy brought Mommy and Ashley home. Aunt Sandy and Uncle Don helped. Everyone fussed over the baby.

"She's so cute,"Aunt Sandy said.

"Adorable," Uncle Don agreed.

"Let me," Stacy said. "Let me hold her. She's *my* sister."

Mommy said, "You can hold her, Big Girl, if you sit on the couch."

Ashley didn't do much while she lay on Stacy's lap. She waved her arms and turned her head. Stacy tickled her feet to see them jump.

"When will she be able to *play* with me?" Stacy asked her daddy.

Daddy said, "Wait and see. She'll grow."

So Stacy waited.

And waited.

And waited.

The grass turned brown and the leaves fell off the trees, and Ashley was still a baby.

"Babies take so looooong to grow," Stacy complained one day. Her voice was muffled because she and Mommy and Daddy were in the middle of a Family Hug. (Stacy was the peanut butter and her parents were the slices of bread.)

"Hey, Big Girl, she's only a few months old. Give her time," her daddy said, laughing. Stacy liked to feel her daddy's rumbling laugh. She liked the tickly feeling on her head where her mother kissed her. She felt safe and happy in the middle of a Family Hug.

Everyone helped take care of the baby. Stacy would hand Daddy a clean diaper when he changed Ashley. "You're such a good big sister," Daddy said. Stacy smiled.

"Since you don't need them anymore, we're using your old diapers for Ashley," Daddy said. Stacy could hardly believe she had ever been as small as Ashley.

They had to figure out a new way to do the Family Hug.

"Let's see," Mother said, arranging Ashley in her arms, "one wonderful Little Girl up here." Ashley wrinkled her tiny nose and sneezed.

"And one wonderful Big Girl down here," Daddy said, smiling at Stacy. "Okay, Family Hug!"

Sometimes Stacy loved the new baby. And sometimes she was angry when her parents spent time taking care of Ashley and didn't pay any attention to her.

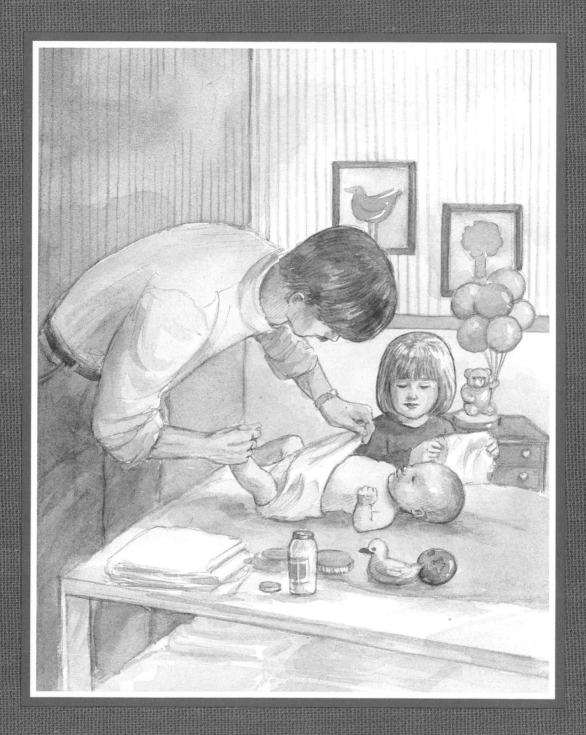

One morning Stacy woke up early. It was still dark, but she could hear the birds twittering to each other in the maple tree outside her window.

She crawled out of bed and wandered down the hall to tell Mommy the birds were keeping her awake. She hoped Mommy was up, taking care of Ashley. Ashley always woke up early.

She heard someone crying. But it didn't sound like Ashley.

Gramma surprised her by coming along behind and scooping Stacy up into her warm, comfortable arms, murmuring, "Oh, Stacy."

Stacy was confused. What was Gramma doing here in the middle of the night?

Gramma carried her to her parents' room, crooning softly.

Daddy sat there looking off into space.

"Stacy," Mommy said. Her voice was so soft Stacy could barely hear it. "Something's . . ." Mommy took a deep breath. "Something's happened to Ashley."

"She died, Stacy," Daddy said. "She died in her sleep."

"Will she wake up?" Stacy asked.

"No, honey," Mommy said. "When a person dies, she doesn't ever wake up."

Stacy didn't know what to say.

She crawled into Mommy's lap. Mommy cradled her tightly.

The next few days were very confusing.

Daddy never laughed his rumbling laugh. Mommy moved slowly around the house.

Friends and relatives came and went. Aunt Sandy hugged Stacy while Uncle Don talked to Mommy and Daddy about something called SIDS.

Sudden Infant Death Syndrome.

Stacy wondered what that was.

Ashley never came back to her crib.

Stacy and Mommy and Daddy went to Ashley's funeral. There were lots of people there.

Stacy didn't understand all the words of the ceremony. All she knew was that Ashley's body was in that box. Daddy said the box was going to be put into the ground next to Grandfather Moore's grave.

That afternoon, Mommy and Daddy helped Stacy put her flowers next to the others where Ashley was buried.

Things changed at home after the funeral.

Mommy cried a lot. Sometimes Daddy did, too.

Mommy yelled at Daddy. Daddy almost stopped talking to anyone, even Stacy.

And Stacy wondered . . .

Did Ashley die because Stacy had been angry that her parents spent so much time with the baby?

Did she die because Stacy had crumpled up her picture?

Did she die because sometimes Stacy had wished Ashley would go away?

Did she die because of something Stacy had said?

Did she die because . . . ?

Did she . . . ?

Stacy wondered.

She was afraid to go to sleep.

Would she wake up?

Or would she get SIDS?

And die?

Stacy didn't like to see Mommy cry. It made her feel awful. One day she crawled up on the couch next to Mommy and began to sniffle.

"What's the matter, Big Girl?" Mommy asked.

"Will I catch SIDS when I go to sleep?"

"Oh, honey," Mommy said. She lifted Stacy up on her lap and hugged her. "You can't catch SIDS. Those are just letters that mean Sudden Infant Death Syndrome. That's doctor–talk for a baby dying without anyone knowing she was going to. Nobody knows why, either."

Mommy paused, resting her chin on Stacy's head. Stacy cuddled deeper into Mommy's arms.

"I miss Ashley," Stacy whispered. "I wish she were still here. She was going to grow up big enough to play with me."

Stacy felt Mommy's tears drip on her hair.

Daddy peeked into the room. "Is this a private hug? Or a Family Hug?" he asked.

"Family Hug, Daddy," Stacy said, reaching for him.

Daddy curved his long arms around the both of them and squeezed. Stacy felt safe and comfortable as the peanut butter between her mommy and daddy. It had been such a long, long time since the last Family Hug. But it wasn't the same without Ashley.

"You won't get SIDS, Stacy," Mommy said. "Only babies do. You're too old to get it."

"Hey, not to worry, Big Girl," Daddy said. "Once you were tiny and helpless, too. Then you grew strong and wonderful, just like most children do. But Ashley was different."

"But . . ." Stacy asked, "Did I make her die? Did I tickle her too hard? Did I . . . ?"

"No, no, no," said Mommy, kissing Stacy's forehead. "Sometimes babies die, no matter how well parents—and big sisters—take care of them." She squeezed Stacy and Daddy in the Family Hug again.

That night, Stacy wasn't afraid to go to sleep.

Several days later Stacy helped Daddy sort through the photographs he had taken of Ashley.

"Can I have this one?" Stacy asked. She held up a picture of herself holding Ashley on her lap.

"Of course you may, Big Girl," he said. "I think we have a frame just the right size for it, too."

Stacy loved the photograph. She put it on her dresser where she could see it from her bed. Every night as she drifted off to sleep she whispered goodnight to it.

And Stacy knew she would always remember her special little sister, Ashley.

1005409642